Bramble and Be[...]

The fox cub peered nerv[...] [thr]ough the long grass. He stared at the kitten's dark, stripy face and her long white whiskers. He had been watching her for a while. She looked very fierce, especially when she had pounced on that piece of straw. *Please don't pounce on me too*, the cub thought, trembling with fear . . .

Skipper and Sky

Sky blinked. Now she could see the deep blue sea stretching away into the distance.

"Isn't it amazing?" Skipper woofed, his tail wagging madly.

Sky pressed her pink nose against the window. She looked out at the endless, shining waves. "Oh, I really wish I could go to sea!" she mewed softly.

Skipper stopped wagging his tail. Had Sky said that she wanted to go to sea? No, he must have got that wrong. Cats didn't like water!

RMK

More Best Friends follow soon!

Best ♥ Friends

A Best Friends Two-Books-in-one Special!

Bramble and Berry

Skipper and Sky

by Jenny Dale

Illustrated by Susan Hellard

A Working Partners Book

MACMILLAN CHILDREN'S BOOKS

Bramble and Berry first published 2002 by Macmillan Children's Books
Skipper and Sky first published 2002 by Macmillan Children's Books
a division of Macmillan Publishers Limited
20 New Wharf Road, London N1 9RR
Basingstoke and Oxford
www.panmacmillan.com

Associated companies throughout the world

Created by Working Partners Limited
London W6 0QT

ISBN 0 330 415042

1 3 5 7 9 8 6 4 2

A CIP catalogue record for this book is available from
the British Library.

Typeset by SX Composing DTP, Rayleigh, Essex
Printed and bound in Great Britain by Mackays of Chatham plc, Kent

Bramble and Berry

Special thanks to Jill Atkins

chapter one

"Look at me!" Bramble dug her sharp claws into the wooden beam, high in the barn. She peered down at her mum, Tabitha.

"Bramble, come down at once," mewed Tabitha. "You'll fall!"

"But it's such fun up here," the kitten miaowed. "I can see lots of exciting things!" She loved looking up at the birds' nests high in the eaves. And she could even see mice scuttling about among the bales of straw below.

"It's all right, Mum," she purred. "I'm quite safe."

At that moment, Bramble felt her paws slipping. She tried to dig her claws deeper. Too late! "Oops!" she wailed as she fell.

The air whistled through Bramble's whiskers and ruffled her furry coat. Halfway down, Bramble flipped her body the right way up and landed paws first in a deep pile of straw.

Tabitha trotted over to her. "You must be more careful," she miaowed, giving Bramble a lick. "You'll get into real trouble one day."

Bramble loved the feel of her mum's rough tongue rasping over her face. "Don't worry about me," she purred.

She lifted her head so Tabitha could reach under her chin.

When Tabitha had finished, Bramble leaped up and scampered out into the farmyard. It was a breezy day. A piece of straw blew along the ground in front of her. Bramble pounced on it, feeling it crackle under her front paws.

A sharp gust of wind blew the straw just out of reach. It fluttered away across the yard.

"Come back," Bramble hissed, bounding after it.

Suddenly, she stopped. A pair of dark, shiny eyes stared at her from the long grass at the edge of the yard.

Bramble crept a little nearer. She saw a thin, red face, a shiny, black nose and two very pointed ears.

It was a fox!

Bramble stood very still. She remembered what her mum had taught her. "Foxes are very dangerous. You must run away if you ever see one."

Shaking all over, Bramble began to back away slowly. She hoped the fox

would not come after her.

The fox cub peered nervously through the long grass. He stared at the kitten's dark, stripy face and her long, white whiskers. He had been watching her for a while. She looked very fierce, especially when she had pounced on that piece of straw. *Please don't pounce on me, too*, the cub thought, trembling with fear.

Bramble noticed the grass quivering. The fox was shivering. "Is he frightened of *me*?" she wondered. Bramble narrowed her eyes and took a closer look. "He's very small," she miaowed. "I'm not scared of *him*!"

Feeling very brave, she stepped forward, arched her back and hissed loudly. "Go away, fox!" she spat.

"Help!" whined the cub. In a panic, he dashed out of the long grass, past the kitten and across the farmyard.

Bramble saw a flash of red fur as the tiny fox shot by. Then she blinked. The fox had disappeared. "I frightened a fox!" she miaowed in surprise.

Bramble scampered to the farmhouse. She stood on her hind legs and pushed her head through the cat flap. "Mum!" she mewed. "I frightened a fox. I scared it right away!"

"A fox?" miaowed Tabitha anxiously, hurrying towards her. "Are you all right?"

"Oh yes," Bramble purred proudly. "We won't see him round here again!"

The fox cub headed for the barn. It was gloomy inside, but he could see a pile of straw in one corner. It would be a good place to hide. He dived into the straw and lay there panting and shaking.

There were strange noises all around him, rustling and fluttering. His heart thumped. He huddled down in the straw, hoping that his mum would come and find him very soon.

Suddenly, the fox cub heard another sound. From his hiding place, he saw a boy enter the barn and walk towards the pile of straw.

"Hello!" said the boy. "There's something hiding in here."

The little fox whined. He pushed his nose deeper into the straw and closed his eyes, hoping the boy wouldn't come any closer. But then he felt a hand stroking his back.

"I don't believe it!" said the boy. "It's a fox cub."

The cub felt the boy's hands lifting him up. He was too frightened to struggle. "Help!" he whimpered.

"Poor thing," said the boy, kindly.

"Are you lost? Don't worry, I'll look after you. I'd better take you indoors."

The boy's quiet voice comforted the fox. He didn't feel quite so scared as the boy carried him out of the barn.

A woman was standing at the farmhouse door. "Hi, Mark," she called. "What have you got there?"

"A fox cub," the boy replied. "Can I keep him?"

The woman hurried over. "He's very tiny," she said. "He'll need careful looking after until we find his mum." She took the cub and stroked him.

The fox cub was not shaking quite so much now. These people had gentle hands and voices. Maybe they would take him back to his mum. He snuggled

into the woman's jumper as she carried
him into the farmhouse. Then he
pricked up his ears and stared around,
his eyes wide. He was in a big room,
which was cool and quiet after the hot,
dusty farmyard.

The woman put the fox down on a soft
blanket. She filled a bowl with water and

put it beside him. The cub looked at the water. He was really thirsty. Slowly, he crept forward to the bowl and began to drink.

Bramble was tucking into some crunchy biscuits when Mark and Mrs Gates came in. Out of the corner of her eye, she spotted a bushy, red tail. She stopped eating and watched the fox cub drink some water.

"What's *he* doing in here?" she hissed. "I thought I got rid of him."

"I think I'll call him Berry," she heard Mark say.

"Berry suits him," said Mrs Gates. "He's the right colour."

Bramble jumped up. "I'm going to frighten that fox away again!" she miaowed. She began to gallop across the kitchen.

Berry saw the stripy-faced creature racing towards him. "Oh no!" he whined. "Here comes that fierce cat again!"

Chapter 2

"What are you doing here?" Bramble hissed. She arched her back.

Berry pressed his nose into the blanket. "Please don't hurt me," he whined.

Bramble felt confused as she looked at the trembling fox. She didn't know what her mum was making such a fuss about. Foxes weren't scary at all!

Tabitha came and stood behind Bramble. "Well!" she miaowed. "So this is the fox you frightened away!"

"Yes, Mum," Bramble purred proudly.

"I hadn't realized it was so small," mewed Tabitha.

Bramble rubbed her head against her mum's face. "Aren't all foxes like this, then?" she asked.

"Oh, no," Tabitha replied. "Grown-up foxes are much bigger. This is only a very young cub. No wonder he's scared."

Berry wanted to hide from the stripy-faced kitten. And there was an even *bigger* cat with her. He tugged at the blanket and tried to wriggle underneath it. The edge of the blanket twitched. In a flash, the kitten pounced on it and began to drag the blanket off him.

Berry growled, "Let go!" He grabbed

the other end between his teeth and
pulled. The more Berry pulled at one
end, the harder the kitten tugged at the
other.

Finally, Berry gave up. He lay still,
panting heavily, his heart pounding in
his chest. "I want my mum," he
whimpered sadly.

The kitten came and sat down beside

him. "Why don't you want to play with me?" she miaowed.

At that moment, the woman hurried over and stroked the kitten. "Now then, Bramble, you fierce little monster," she said. "Leave our visitor alone."

The kitten purred and rubbed her head against the woman's hand. Then she trotted away.

Berry sniffed and sat up. What was that delicious smell? He crouched down as the boy loomed over him and put a dish on the floor. Berry sniffed again. He didn't know what was in the dish, but it smelled very tasty! He stepped forward and took a mouthful. Yum! He gulped down all the food and then had another drink of water.

After that he felt much better. He crept
back to the blanket and lay on his side
with his tail stretched out across the
floor. He could keep an eye on the two
cats from there. They were eating some
food as well.

Bramble had nearly finished. She
watched Berry over the top of her dish.
"You look a bit lonely," she mewed. She

quickly washed her whiskers, then jumped up and scampered across the room towards the fox cub.

Berry's heart beat faster as he watched the kitten racing towards him. What was she going to do this time? To his surprise, Bramble stopped, reached out her paw and tapped the tip of his tail.

Berry jumped up and swished his tail behind him. "What are you doing?" he yapped crossly.

But Bramble didn't answer. Instead, she gently patted his nose. Berry blinked, then he tried to pat Bramble back. But she dodged away and raced across the kitchen.

"Come back!" Berry called.

"I bet you can't catch me!" miaowed

Bramble playfully.

Berry set off after Bramble. He tried
to catch up with her as she scampered
under the table, but it wasn't easy. His
paws skidded on the slippery floor. It
wasn't like the soft ground in the woods
where he lived.

Berry chased Bramble round and
round the kitchen, sliding around
corners and bumping into the table legs.
His ears flapped madly and his tail
streamed out behind him. The faster he
ran, the more excited he got. This was
fun!

Suddenly, Bramble stopped. Berry
crashed into her with a bump. They fell
over and landed in a heap.

Berry looked at Bramble. She wasn't at

all scary, really. She was soft and furry, and she was out of breath, just like him.

Bramble sat up. "I'm thirsty," she mewed. "Do you want a drink?"

"Yes, I do," yapped Berry.

They trotted to the water bowl and, side by side, they began to lap the cool water.

As soon as it was light, Bramble leaped over the side of the basket and l... across the kitch...

That night, Berry curle...
blanket. He tried hard to get to...
but strange humming and clicking noises
kept him awake. He missed his mum
and his den in the woods, and he
whimpered quietly in the darkness.
Luckily, he could hear Bramble and
Tabitha purring. It made him feel
better to know that Bramble was nearby.
She might even help him find his mum
in the morning. Berry started to feel
sleepy at last.

bounded

chen floor. "Berry!" she mewed as she skidded to a halt in front of the blanket. "Are you awake?"

There was no reply, so Bramble craned her neck over the edge of the blanket. She saw a bundle of red fur, two pointed ears and a nose tucked under a white-tipped tail. Berry was fast asleep.

"Come on, lazy bones!" Bramble miaowed, more loudly. "I'm ready to play."

Berry blinked and sat up, looking at Bramble with his head on one side. He yawned. He didn't feel like playing yet. He still felt very sleepy.

Bramble leaped on to the blanket,
bounced off again and raced across the
floor, but Berry didn't move. Bramble
scampered back and began tugging a
corner of the blanket. "It's time to play,"
she miaowed.

Berry slowly stood up and stretched.
He watched Bramble scamper over to
a little yellow ball. She tapped it so it

rolled towards Berry, then she chased it and tapped it again. The ball rolled temptingly across the smooth floor.

Berry bounded off the blanket and raced after the ball. He snatched it up in his mouth, then he shook his head and the ball flew in the air. But as he ran after it again, he felt Bramble's paws grab him. He tumbled on to his side with a grunt.

Bramble pounced on him again and they rolled over and over together on the kitchen floor. She could feel Berry's tickly fur under her paws. She playfully batted his ears, keeping her claws tucked in. "I told you I was going to cheer you up," she panted. "Come on. I'll show you what else we can do."

The door into the sitting room was open. Bramble squeezed through the gap and trotted boldly over to the curtains. "Watch this!" she mewed, digging her claws into the thick, soft material. Up and up she climbed, until Berry looked like a tiny ball of red fluff far below. Suddenly, the door opened and Mrs Gates and Mark came in.

"Bramble!" exclaimed Mrs Gates, lifting her down. "You'll ruin my curtains, you wicked kitten."

But Bramble wasn't listening. She gave a big wriggle and jumped out of Mrs Gates's arms. As soon as her paws touched the carpet, she raced off with Berry close behind her. There was a lovely, thick rug on the other side of the

room. It had fluffy tassels on one end.
Bramble loved playing with them. She
sprang on to the tassels and pulled.

Berry crouched next to her and tugged
a tassel hard with his teeth.

"Bramble!" called Mark, laughing and
clapping his hands. "Stop teaching
Berry all your naughty tricks." He
shooed them away from the rug, back
into the kitchen.

As soon as Berry entered the room, he
smelled something delicious. Food! He
lifted his nose and sniffed the air. The
tempting smell was coming from
something on the table. Berry thought
for a moment. If he could just pull that
cloth off the table, the dish might fall on
to the floor beside him. He reached up

and held the edge of the tablecloth in his mouth.

"Stop!" shouted Mark, grabbing the cloth.

Berry let go and dived under the table, where Bramble was waiting for him.

"Bad luck," Bramble mewed, nudging him with her head. Then she heard a familiar rattling sound. "Don't worry, Berry," she miaowed. "I can hear Mark getting my lunch ready. Crunchy biscuits, yum!"

After lunch, Bramble and Berry curled up together on Berry's blanket and had a snooze. Berry woke up first. He had been asleep for ages, and now he felt full of energy. He jumped up and trotted

over to the door. There was a little
square flap in it that he hadn't noticed
before.

Berry pressed his nose against it and
felt his tummy flip over with excitement.
He could smell damp grass and leafy
trees. The woods! He butted the flap
with his head. It swung open, and Berry
caught a glimpse of the farmyard
through the little gap.

"Bramble, wake up!" he yapped.

Bramble uncurled and sat up. "What's
the matter, Berry?" she mewed sleepily.

"I've found a little door," Berry
barked. "I think it leads outside."

"That's my cat flap," Bramble mewed.
"Watch." She ran over to Berry. Then
she stood on her hind legs and pushed

her nose against the swinging door. As it opened, she wriggled through the hole. The last thing Berry saw was a flick of her fluffy tail. Then she was gone.

Suddenly, the cat flap swung towards him and Bramble's face appeared. "Come on," she miaowed. "It's easy." Then she disappeared again.

Berry nervously touched the flap with his nose.

"Hurry up!" called Bramble from outside.

Berry didn't find it very easy at all. He pushed and wriggled and scrabbled with his back paws. The sides of the little doorway brushed against his fur. At last he slithered out into the farmyard. But the flap swung back down and hit him on the bottom!

"Ouch!" he yelped, jumping to his paws. Then he stopped. What was that loud roaring noise? Bramble flattened his ears and looked around wildly.

Just then, a big red thing thundered into the farmyard, making the loudest noise Berry had ever heard.

chapter 4

Bramble watched as Berry shot like an
arrow back through the cat flap. She
bounded after him, and found him
huddled in his blanket. He was trembling
from the end of his nose to the tip of his
bushy tail.

Bramble licked his fur. "What's the
matter?" she purred in surprise.

"Th-that red thing," Berry
whimpered. "It s-scared me."

"It's only a tractor!" Bramble
miaowed. How could Berry be scared

of a silly old tractor?

"W-what's a t-t-tractor?" Berry yelped.

"Mr Gates uses it to ride all over the
farm," Bramble explained. "It won't
hurt you. Come on."

Berry's paws were still shaking as he
left his comfy blanket and followed
Bramble through the cat flap again.
It was easier to get through this time.
Berry was very glad to see that the
red tractor was chugging back out of
the gate.

"This way," miaowed Bramble as she
scampered across the farmyard.

Berry followed close behind her. She
led him under the fence and into a wide,
green field. Berry felt a shiver of
excitement down his back. He had been

in this field before. On the far side were
some trees.

Berry paused and sniffed. He knew
where he was! Those trees were at the
edge of the woods where he used to live.
Maybe his mum was somewhere in
there. He hurtled past Bramble and
dashed up the field towards the trees.

"Wait for me!" Bramble called, but
Berry was in too much of a hurry.

Suddenly, a brightly coloured butterfly
fluttered past his nose, tickling him with
its velvety wings. Berry leaped up and
tried to catch it, but it flew away. A sweet
smell filled his nose. He looked down at
his paws and saw lots of little flowers all
around him. He burrowed his nose into
the flowers and rolled in the grass. The

sun made his fur glow warmly and a gentle breeze ruffled his ears. It was great to be outside again!

Just then, he heard Mark calling. "Bramble! Berry! Where are you? It's supper time!"

"Yummy!" Berry yapped. "I'm hungry." He began to trot back down

the field. He looked round for Bramble, but he couldn't see her anywhere.

Bramble had been chasing a baby rabbit. She had followed it right to the top of the field before the rabbit disappeared down a hole. Bramble looked around and realized she was very close to the woods. She could smell lots of exciting scents coming from the trees. "This might be a good place to explore," she mewed, trotting nearer.

She stopped at the edge of the woods and peered through the thick green leaves. It looked rather dark under the trees, but Bramble didn't mind. She felt very brave. With her whiskers twitching and ears pricked, she stepped under the fence and into the woods.

A big, black beetle scuttled across her path. It was smooth and shiny. Bramble reached out to touch it, but it slid under a leaf and disappeared out of sight.

Something tickled her head. Bramble looked up. A spider was hanging from its fine thread just above her. The tiny creature swung to and fro in the breeze.

Bramble was just about to reach up, when there was a strange snuffling sound behind her. She whipped round and pounced.

"Ouch!" she yowled, springing away from the prickly thing. She watched, her eyes very wide, as the spiky ball slowly uncurled. A pointed black nose and two tiny black eyes appeared from the middle of the prickles. Then the strange

animal shuffled off into the bushes.

Bramble shook her tingling paws and
decided not to chase after it. She walked
further into the woods. A cold breeze
ruffled her fur and she shivered. It was
starting to get dark. Perhaps it wasn't
such a good idea to come into the woods
on her own.

"I'd better go back to the farm now,"

she miaowed to herself.

But which way was home? Bramble couldn't remember. She peered round, but all the trees looked the same. Never mind. She would soon find the way.

Bramble squeezed between two large bushes, but she couldn't go any further because there was a very tall tree in the way. She backed out of the bushes and tried another path. It led straight into a clump of very prickly brambles.

Suddenly, a scary hooting sound came from high up in the trees. "Whooo are you?"

Bramble jumped and peered up into the darkness. She couldn't see a thing.

"Whooo?"

What was making that creepy sound?

Bramble narrowed her eyes, but she could only see shadowy branches swaying in the wind.

Bramble realized that she was lost. She crawled under a bush with thick green leaves and thought about home. She began to yowl loudly. "Mum! Berry! Help!"

chapter 5

It was warm and cosy in the kitchen.
Berry crunched up the biscuits that
Mark had put in his bowl. When he had
finished, he licked every last crumb from
around his mouth and nose. Then he
looked at Bramble's bowl, which was
next to his. It was still full. Where had
Bramble got to? She should have been
back by now.

Berry trotted to the cat flap and looked
through it. It was nearly dark outside.
"Bramble!" he yapped. "Where are you?"

He was ready for a nap on his blanket, but he couldn't settle down while he was worried about his friend. He had to go and find Bramble. He jumped out through the cat flap, ran across the farmyard and peered through the fence. He couldn't see Bramble anywhere.

Berry walked into the field and stared up at the woods. The sound of the wind in the leaves made him feel safe. But Berry knew it would be a dangerous place for a kitten at night.

"Oh, Bramble!" he whined. "Where have you gone?" He trotted across the field. "Bramble!" he called a bit louder. "Can you hear me?" He stopped to listen, but there was no answer.

"I'll have to go into the woods to look for her," he yapped.

As he stepped under the trees, Berry lifted his nose and sniffed the familiar woodland smells. A gentle breeze smoothed his fur. He was home!

"Whooo?" came a call from above his head.

Berry looked up. "Hello, owl!" he barked. "I've come home!"

Deep in the woods, Bramble huddled in her hiding place under the bush. She was feeling very scared. The noises of the night seemed to close in around her, rustling and hissing and hooting.

Suddenly, she heard a loud bark not far away. Bramble jumped. Her tail fluffed up and she opened her eyes very wide. What if that was a *grown-up* fox? Now Bramble didn't feel brave at all.

"Help!" she yowled. "I want to go home!"

Berry pricked up his ears. He could hear a faint cry in the distance. "Bramble!" he yapped as loudly as he could. "Is that you?"

Bramble held her breath and watched the shadows. They were full of dark, spooky shapes. Something brushed against her back. She whipped round, but it was only a branch. She pricked up her ears, straining to hear the scary bark again. But all she could hear was a tiny yapping sound. It didn't sound scary. It sounded very familiar.

Bramble sat up. "Berry!" she miaowed at the top of her voice. "I'm here! Help!"

Berry heard Bramble's cry very clearly. "Hooray!" he yapped. "I've found her!" He bounded through the bushes towards the sound. "Don't be afraid, Bramble," he barked bravely into the dark woods. "I'm coming!"

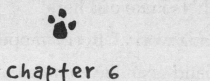

chapter 6

Bramble sat bolt upright. Berry had
come to rescue her! She leaped out from
under the bush. "Berry!" she yowled.
"I'm over here!"

Suddenly, Berry bounded into the
clearing from behind a tree. His fur
gleamed like silver in the moonlight. He
galloped towards her with his tail
stretched out behind him.

On shaky paws, Bramble raced over to
him. "Thank goodness you found me,"
she purred, burying her nose in his thick

fur. "It's so scary in here!"

"Don't worry," Berry yapped, licking his friend's ear. "I've come to take you home. Come on." He turned and set off through the wood. After a few steps, he stopped and looked round. Bramble was so close behind, she bumped into his tail. Her eyes were very wide and her fur was fluffed up. Berry felt sorry for her. *The woods must seem very spooky to her*, he thought.

Bramble kept as close to Berry as she could as they trotted through the woods. She couldn't wait to get home. "Thank you for coming to find me," she mewed. "I was really scared."

Suddenly, a dark, slinky shape stepped on to the path. Bramble saw a long,

narrow face and bright black eyes. Sharp
white teeth glinted in the darkness.

Bramble stopped dead. Then she
arched her back and spat. "Berry," she
hissed. "Look out!"

Berry looked up. But he didn't seem
scared at all. Instead, he let out a cry
of delight. "Mum!" he yapped, leaping
up and licking the animal's face. "Where

have you been?"

"Everywhere," barked Berry's mum. She gently nuzzled him with her nose. "I've been looking all over the woods for you. I thought I'd *never* find you."

Berry felt bubbles of happiness fizzing inside him. He had come into the woods to rescue Bramble and now he had found his mum as well! He pushed his nose into his mum's lovely, warm fur and smelled her familiar scent. "I've missed you, Mum," he mumbled.

Bramble watched Berry and his mum making a fuss of each other. She could feel her fur bristling on the back of her neck. It was scary being this close to a grown-up fox! Her teeth looked very sharp, and she was much, much bigger

than Bramble, or even Bramble's mum.
Bramble inched backwards under a
bush.

"Hey, Bramble," yapped Berry,
hurrying towards her. "Why are you
hiding? There's nothing to be scared of."

Bramble crept slowly forward, keeping
her eyes on the big fox's face.

Berry's mum stared down at her.

"Who's this?" she asked.

"It's Bramble," yapped Berry.

Bramble took a deep breath. Her heart was hammering so loud, she thought Berry's mum must be able to hear it. "Hello," she mewed.

Berry ran over to Bramble and pressed his body against her fur. "Bramble looked after me," he explained to his mum. "She cheered me up when I was lost, and she played with me, and now we're best friends."

"Thank you, Bramble," Berry's mum barked kindly. "But what are you doing in the woods at night?"

Bramble went a few steps nearer. "I was exploring," she miaowed. "But I got lost. Berry came to find me."

"And now I'm taking her back to the farm," yapped Berry.

His mum frowned. "We should stay in the woods," she barked. "It's safer for us in here."

"But we ought to take her to the fence on the other side of the field," Berry protested. He wanted to make sure that Bramble got safely back to *her* mum, now that he had found his.

"All right," replied his mum. "But we must take care."

Berry and his mum set off through the woods, following an invisible path between the bushes. Bramble trotted quietly behind them. They soon reached the edge of the trees. Across the field, the lights from the farmhouse twinkled

51

in the darkness. Bramble sighed happily.
She couldn't wait to see her mum again,
and the lovely warm kitchen. *And* she
hadn't had any supper!

She dashed out of the trees and across
the field with Berry and his mum racing
beside her.

When they had almost reached the

farm, Berry's mum stopped. "Stay here, son," she barked quietly. "We mustn't go any further."

Bramble and Berry banged into each other as they skidded to a halt. They rolled over and over in the long, wet grass.

Berry rubbed his head against Bramble's soft kitten fur. "But Mum!" he whined, sitting up. "I'll miss Bramble."

"I'll miss you, too," Bramble purred. Just then, she smelled the straw from the barn and heard the chickens clucking in the yard. "But I do want to go home!" she added.

"It's time for us to go," barked Berry's mum.

Bramble nuzzled against Berry's

pointed face. "Will you come and visit me again soon?" she purred sadly.

"Yes, lots," Berry promised. "But I can't come into the farmyard any more. It's not safe for foxes."

"And I'd better not go up to the woods again!" mewed Bramble. "They're scary!"

"But we could meet in this field," Berry yapped.

"OK!" Bramble purred. "That's a good idea."

Berry and his mum turned towards the woods, their long tails swishing against the grass.

Bramble felt sad as she watched them slip away into the night. She would miss Berry very much, but she was really glad he had found his mum.

"See you soon!" she called as the white tip of Berry's tail disappeared into the darkness. Then she jumped through the fence and ran towards the farmhouse.

Skipper and Sky

Special thanks to Narinder Dhami

Chapter one

"I wish I could go to sea!" Sky mewed.
The silver tabby kitten sat down on the
harbour wall and flicked her tail from
side to side. Big green waves splashed
against the wall below her. Drops of
white spray clung to her whiskers,
making her fur tingle.

Sky loved the sea. She lived with her
owner, Joe, and his family in a cottage
right beside the harbour. More than
anything else, Sky wanted to go on a boat,
out of the harbour and across the sea.

She looked at the fishing-boats bobbing up and down on the sparkling water. The fishermen were getting ready to leave. Sky could see Joe on the long wooden jetty that stood on legs above the sea at one side of the harbour. He was helping his father to fold up the nets. Joe's dad was a fisherman, and his boat was called the *Jolly Jack*.

"Joe's dad is so lucky," thought Sky. "He can go out in his boat whenever he wants!"

"Hello, Sky." Joe caught sight of her and waved.

Sky blinked her special cat greeting and jumped down from the harbour wall. As she padded over to see him, she lifted her pink nose and sniffed the salty air. It was early in the day, but the sun already felt warm on Sky's thick fur. Sky purred loudly, thinking of all the tasty fish Joe's dad would catch today. "This is the best place to live in the whole world!" she mewed happily.

Sky sat up and sniffed the air again. She could smell something new. She turned round to see what it was.

A man and a puppy were walking along the path to the harbour. The man had a round, friendly face and a grey beard. The puppy's coat was dark brown and very scruffy, and he had big brown eyes.

Joe's dad waved at the man. "Hello, Mac," he called. "Hello, Skipper."

"Hello, Mr Kirby," called Mac.

"Lovely day today, isn't it? I wish I was going out on the boats with you!"

Joe's dad smiled. "You haven't met my son yet, have you?" he went on. "Joe, this is Mac, the new lighthouse keeper."

Sky jumped up as Joe went over to meet Mac. She wanted to say hello too!

The puppy watched, his dark eyes bright and eager, as Sky padded over. "Hello," he woofed, wagging his tail. "I'm Skipper. I live in the lighthouse."

"Hello," Sky mewed. "I'm Sky." She stretched her neck to stare at the tall red-and-white tower on the headland beyond the little harbour. She had never been to the lighthouse, but she had always been curious about the enormous tower. Sky knew that it had a big light

which flashed on and off when it was
dark or foggy. But she didn't know what
the light was for. "Do you really live
there?" she asked.

"Oh, yes," Skipper barked. "Looking
after the lighthouse is a very important
job!"

Sky opened her eyes wide. She liked
Skipper. The puppy was very friendly –

his tail never stopped wagging! She was just about to ask him what the lighthouse was for, when Mac called to his puppy.

"Come on, Skipper," he said. "Let's go and collect that light bulb."

"OK, Mac," Skipper woofed. He turned to Sky. "We're picking up a new bulb for the lighthouse," he explained.

"Maybe I'll see you later," Sky mewed. She watched as Skipper followed Mac to the post office on the other side of the harbour.

"Sky?" Joe's dad called from the boat. "Look what I've found!" He held up a plump, silver fish.

Sky purred and scampered down the jetty towards the boat. The wood felt smooth and warm under her paws. Mr Kirby threw the fish to her, and Sky caught it neatly. Then she ran off and hid behind some crab pots to eat it.

"Lovely!" she mumbled through a mouthful of tasty fish. When she had finished, she washed herself from her ears to the tip of her tail. "That's my *favourite* breakfast. My favourite lunch and dinner too!"

The fishing-boats were ready to leave. Sky padded out from behind the crab pots and stared out to sea. Sunshine sparkled on the water, and the waves were tipped with white foam. Sky couldn't imagine anything better than being in a boat on a day like today. Bobbing up and down on the shimmering sea.

She looked around. Mr Kirby and Joe were talking to one of the other fishermen. This was her chance! Her heart thumping with excitement, Sky padded over to the *Jolly Jack* and jumped on board.

She hunted around for a good place to

sit. On the other side of the deck there was a pile of fishy smelling nets that looked very comfy. Sky climbed on top of them, sat down and tucked her paws underneath her. She began to purr loudly, imagining the adventure ahead of her. The boat would skim over the waves in the warm sun. There would be a cool, salty breeze as they sped along. The nets would be thrown into the water, and would soon be full of silver fish. Sky purred even louder. She would be able to eat as many fish as she liked!

Suddenly, two big hands grabbed her round her furry tummy and lifted her into the air. Sky yowled crossly.

"Look what I've found," Joe's dad laughed.

"Put me down!" the kitten mewed, wriggling. "I'm going to sea!"

"Has she tried to come on board again?" laughed one of the other fishermen. "She hid in that empty crab pot last time, remember?"

"Sky, don't you know that cats are supposed to hate water?" Joe sighed. He came over to take the kitten from his dad, and rubbed his cheek on the top of her head. "Why do you keep trying to get on Dad's boat?"

"Because I want to go to sea," Sky mewed, peering over Joe's shoulder as he carried her back down the jetty. She watched sadly as the fishing-boats chugged out of the harbour. Why *couldn't* she go with them? It wasn't fair!

chapter two

"Come on, Mac," Skipper barked. He trotted out of the shop, his tail wagging madly. He was very excited because Mac had just collected a new bulb for the lighthouse. The bulb was very big, and it was packed in a huge cardboard box.

"Don't get under my feet, Skipper," Mac panted, as hc carried the box out of the post office.

"I won't," Skipper woofed. "Just watch out you don't drop the light bulb!"

They began to walk back to the car

park. Skipper watched Mac all the time to make sure he didn't trip over anything.

Skipper looked round the harbour. Most of the fishing-boats had gone, and Joe had gone too. So had the kitten who had been sitting on the wall. Skipper felt a bit disappointed. Sky had seemed very friendly.

"Good morning," Mac said to a man selling ice cream. He put the box down on the ground and stopped to have a chat.

Skipper began to sniff his way down the wooden jetty. It was full of interesting smells. A fisherman was mending a net at the far end of the jetty. Skipper thought about saying hello, but

the fisherman looked a bit grumpy. So
the puppy kept away from him.

There was another net lying on the
ground. Skipper sniffed his way over to
it.

"Are you coming, Skipper?" Mac
called from the end of the jetty. He had
picked up the box and was ready to go.

Skipper was about to run back to his
owner when he stopped. What was that?
There was something moving in the net!
He padded over to take a closer look.

"I'll see you back at home, Skipper,"
Mac called, and got in the car to drive
back with the bulb. He knew that
Skipper loved to run back across the
cliffs to the lighthouse – it wasn't far.

Skipper prodded the net with his paw.

It was rolled up in a big heap, and he couldn't see what was inside. He hoped the moving thing wasn't a crab. They had very sharp, snappy claws.

He pushed his nose into the net and sniffed. "Who's there?" he woofed. It didn't smell like a fish at all. It smelt like a cat!

"HELP!" Sky yowled. She was very cross. She had been trying to reach a tasty piece of fish in the middle of the net, when the net had wrapped itself around her legs and her tail. She had tried to pull herself free, but the more Sky struggled, the more she got tangled up. The net had wrapped round her tighter and tighter. Now she was well and truly stuck.

Skipper pushed at the net with his nose. "Is that you, Sky?" he barked. He could just see the kitten's tail twitching. "It's me, Skipper."

"I'm stuck!" Sky wailed. She wriggled about until she could turn her head and look up at the puppy. "Please help me!"

"Of course I will," Skipper woofed.

He tried to pull the net away with his paw, but it was too heavy. Then he had another idea. "Keep still," he told Sky.

Skipper bent his head and began to bite one corner of the net. If he could chew a small hole, then the kitten could squeeze out. The net wasn't easy to break, but Skipper's teeth were strong.

Sky watched the puppy chewing away at the net. Her heart was thumping. What would she do if Skipper couldn't get her out? But soon Skipper had made a tiny hole in the net. The hole grew bigger and bigger. Sky felt the net beginning to loosen around her.

"Try now," Skipper woofed.

Sky began to squeeze through the hole. It was quite a tight fit. She puffed and panted as she pushed herself through. The net tugged at her fur, and it felt like she was going to get tangled up again. But at last she squeezed out of the hole, and landed on the jetty beside Skipper's paws.

"Are you all right?" Skipper asked, giving her a gentle nudge with his nose.

"Yes, I'm fine," Sky purred. "Thank you for helping me."

"That's OK," Skipper woofed. He looked down at Sky, who was busy grooming her ruffled fur. Skipper hadn't made any friends yet because he and Mac had only moved into the lighthouse a few days ago. Maybe Sky could be his very first friend!

Just then they heard an angry shout

from behind them.

"Hey! What have you done to my net?"

Sky and Skipper spun round. The grumpy fisherman was running towards them. He looked even more grumpy now!

"Quick!" Skipper woofed. "Let's get out of here!"

The kitten and the puppy raced off down the jetty. The fisherman chased after them, puffing and panting. "Leave my nets alone!" he yelled.

Skipper raced along the path that led from the harbour towards the lighthouse. Sky followed him, running as fast as she could. They ran all the way across the cliff path and didn't stop until

they got to the lighthouse. Then they
looked back to see if the fisherman was
still chasing them. He was nowhere to be
seen.

"I think we're safe!" Sky puffed.
She turned and stared up at the
red-and-white tower looming over them.
She had to crane her neck right back to
see the top. "I've never been all the way

to the lighthouse before," she mewed in
a small voice. "It's *enormous*!"

Skipper wagged his tail hard. "It's
great, isn't it?" he woofed. "Why don't
you come inside and have a look
round?"

chapter three

Skipper trotted up some stone steps and through the front door of the lighthouse. Sky followed him inside, then stopped dead. There was a spiral staircase in front of her. The stairs seemed to go on forever! Round and round and round, higher and higher and higher.

"Come on," called Skipper.

Sky looked around curiously as she followed. The bottom part of the lighthouse was where Skipper and Mac lived. There was a kitchen and a bedroom and a sitting room. To Sky's surprise, all the rooms were curved, without any corners!

Mac was in the sitting room, unpacking a big cardboard box.

"This is the new bulb for the lighthouse lamp," Skipper told Sky. "The old one will need replacing soon."

Sky watched Mac lift the huge glass bulb out of the box. "It's very big," she mewed. It was about the size of a football. Sky could see her reflection in the glass. It was stretched into a funny shape, so that her face looked really wide and her legs looked long and skinny.

"It has to be big," Skipper woofed, "so that the fishermen can see it when they're out at sea. When they see the flashing light, they know they shouldn't get too close. They can keep away from the rocks, and sail safely into the harbour."

"Oh!" Sky mewed. "So that's what the lighthouse is for!"

Skipper wagged his tail proudly. "Do you want to come up and see where the bulb goes?" he offered.

"Yes, please," miaowed Sky.

Skipper led the way over to the staircase. Sky stopped at the bottom, feeling a bit worried. "Do we have to go all the way up *there*?" she asked. Just looking at the steps made her dizzy.

"Yes, right to the top!" Skipper barked, turning round and giving her a friendly lick. "Come on up."

He trotted up the stairs, and Sky went after him. They climbed higher and higher and higher. It was a *very* long way. Soon Sky was out of breath and her legs were aching.

"Keep going!" Skipper woofed. "It's not far now."

Sky began to feel very hot. Maybe they were climbing all the way up to the sun!

Just when Sky thought she couldn't climb another step, Skipper turned to her. "Here we are," he announced.

They had reached the top of the tower! At first Sky couldn't see anything because her eyes were dazzled. Bright sunshine was streaming in through huge glass windows all around the tower.

Sky blinked. Now she could see the deep blue sea stretching away into the distance.

"Isn't it amazing?" Skipper woofed, his tail wagging madly.

Sky pressed her pink nose against the window. She looked out at the endless, shining waves. "Oh, I really wish I could go to sea!" she mewed softly.

Skipper stopped wagging his tail. Had Sky said that she wanted to go to sea? No, he must have got that wrong. Cats didn't like water! "What did you say?" he woofed.

Sky turned to the puppy. "I want to go out on the fishing-boat with Joe's dad," she told him. "But every time I get on the boat, he takes me off again."

Skipper's ears went down. "I wouldn't like to go on a boat," he whimpered. "I like being on dry land!"

Sky didn't seem to hear him. She had pressed her nose to the window again. "Look, Skipper," she mewed. "The fishing-boats are coming back."

Skipper and Sky watched the boats

chugging over the water. They looked tiny from high up in the lighthouse. Sky suddenly felt very hungry as she thought about all of the fish they would be bringing back.

"I have to go and help Joe's dad," Sky mewed to Skipper. "Thank you for showing me the lighthouse. Bye!" And she ran off down the stairs.

"Sky! Wait!" Skipper barked.

Sky stopped on the lighthouse steps. "What's the matter?"

"Can I come with you?" Skipper woofed. "I'd love to watch the boats come in."

"Sure!" Sky purred.

Together they rushed along the cliff path. Just as they reached the harbour,

Sky stopped. Joe was on the jetty, climbing down the ladder to his little rowing-boat. He was carrying his fishing rod and a rucksack. He must be going fishing, Sky thought.

Sky suddenly felt very excited. A very daring idea had popped into her head. "Oh!" she mewed, opening her eyes very wide. "This is my chance to go to sea!"

Skipper turned round. His big brown eyes looked worried. "Are you *sure* you want to go to sea?" he asked. "What if you fall out of the boat? Cats aren't supposed to like water. They belong on dry land."

"I'll be fine," Sky told him. "Joe will look after me. See you later!"

Sky ran over to the boat. She was about to call out to Joe, but then she stopped. "Maybe it's better if I hide," she mewed to herself. "Joe might not let me go otherwise."

Just then Joe turned away to untie the boat. Sky saw her chance. She jumped lightly off the jetty and landed in the boat. Quickly she squeezed under the wooden bench. She peeped out and saw Joe sit down and pick up the oars. Then the boat began to move.

Sky felt very excited. She was on her way to sea at last!

Skipper was standing by the harbour. He saw Sky jump into the boat and hide. Then he watched Joe row the boat away from the jetty.

"Sky's so brave!" Skipper woofed to himself. "Maybe cats *can* go to sea after all . . ."

chapter four

"Hello, Joe!" Sky purred. She crawled out from under the bench and jumped on to Joe's knee. She had stayed hidden until the boat was quite far out to sea. She didn't want Joe to take her back home!

Joe's eyes opened wide. "Sky!" he gasped. "What are *you* doing here?"

"I'm going fishing with you," Sky mewed. "I told you I wanted to go to sea!"

Joe shook his head. "You must really

want to go on a boat," he said, stroking Sky's back. "Well, I can't take you back now. Just make sure you don't fall in!" He began to row again.

Sky sat on the bench next to Joe, feeling very happy. This was as much fun as she had imagined! She loved the way they bobbed up and down on the waves. She loved hearing the water slapping against the sides of the boat. Sky licked her salty whiskers. It would have been even better if Skipper could have come too, she thought. She turned and looked back at the lighthouse. It was getting smaller and smaller as Joe rowed on.

Soon Joe stopped and tied the boat to a bright yellow buoy floating on the water. Then he picked up his fishing rod.

Sky stretched out her front paws in delight. "Fish for lunch," she mewed. "Yum!" She curled up on the bench and yawned, feeling warm and sleepy. Purring happily, she closed her eyes . . .

Back at the lighthouse, Skipper was lying in front of the fire in the sitting room. He couldn't wait for Sky to come back.

He wanted to hear all about her adventure! Skipper yawned and rested his nose on his paws for a snooze.

He woke up with a jump when Mac hurried into the room. He looked worried. Skipper sat up and pricked his ears.

"The lighthouse bulb isn't working," Mac said.

"Oh, no!" Skipper whimpered. His ears went flat and his tail drooped. "We must replace it before it gets dark."

"We need to get the new bulb working quickly," Mac went on. He shook his head, frowning. "It's very foggy out there, and the boats won't be able to see where the rocks are."

"Foggy?" Skipper barked, puzzled. It

hadn't been foggy when he watched Sky
get into Joe's boat.

He trotted out of the lighthouse and
stood at the top of the steps. Mac was
right, it was *very* foggy. Thick, damp
cloud swirled around Skipper, making
his fur cold and wet. He could hardly see
the bottom of the steps, let alone the
beach or the village by the harbour.

Suddenly Skipper began to feel very worried about Sky. Had she and Joe come back yet? Or were they still out at sea, lost in this thick white fog?

chapter five

Sky was eating a very tasty fish. It was the biggest fish she'd ever seen. It was almost as big as she was! "Thank you for catching this fish for me, Joe," she purred.

But something very strange was happening. The more Sky ate, the bigger the fish seemed to get. Sky tried to push the fish away, but it flapped against her fur, cold and wet and heavy . . .

Sky sat up with a jump. She hadn't been eating a fish at all. She'd been asleep, having a dream. But her fur *was* cold and wet. Sky looked around, her green eyes wide with alarm. The boat was surrounded by thick, white fog. It looked as if they were floating in the middle of a cloud.

"Where's the sea gone?" Sky wailed. She jumped to her paws and peered over the edge of the boat at the gloomy grey water. She could just see the buoy that the boat was tied to. But she couldn't see anything else through the fog. How were they going to find their way home?

Sky looked down at Joe, who had fallen asleep in the bottom of the boat. "Wake up, Joe," she mewed, patting his face with her paw.

Joe opened his eyes and sat up. "Goodness, it's all foggy!" he gasped. "Don't worry, Sky," he said, stroking the kitten's head. "The lighthouse will help us to get home. We will be able to find the harbour once we get past the lighthouse and the rocks."

Sky felt a bit happier. Of course! That was what the lighthouse was for. She

looked around, trying to spot the light shining through the fog. But she couldn't see anything.

"That's funny," Joe said. "I can't see the light." He sounded worried. "We'd better try and row back to the shore anyway."

Sky felt even more scared now. She was cold and hungry and she wanted to go home. She watched as Joe untied the boat and picked up the oars. How would Joe know which way to go? Where was the light?

Sky crept over and curled up on the bench next to Joe. The heavy blanket of fog made everything very quiet and spooky. She wished she were at home, sitting in front of the fire. Skipper was right. Cats belong on dry land! "I want to go home," she whimpered.

Joe looked a bit scared, but he started rowing. If he couldn't see the lighthouse, how would they find their way home?

Suddenly Sky's ears pricked up. She could hear something.

There it was again, louder this time. A long, howling cry, as if someone was calling to them through the fog . . .

chapter six

"Sky!" Skipper howled as loudly as he could from the rocks by the lighthouse. "Sky, where are you-oooo?" He put his head on one side and listened hard, but he couldn't hear anything.

He tried again. "Sky, where are you-oooo?"

This time Skipper's ears pricked up. Somewhere in the fog he could hear a boy's voice shouting. He padded forward carefully on the slippery rocks. "Joe! Sky!" he barked. "Is that you?"

Out in the boat, Sky could hardly believe her ears. It was Skipper! "Skipper!" she mewed at the top of her voice. "Where are you?"

"I'm over here," Skipper woofed. "On the rocks near the lighthouse. The bulb isn't working. Mac is trying to replace it with the new one."

So *that* was why they couldn't see the lighthouse, Sky thought.

"Hey! I think I can hear a dog," said Joe, sounding surprised. He put down the oars to listen.

Sky mewed eagerly to try to make Joe understand. Skipper was trying to help!

"Could it be Mac's puppy?" Joe asked. The barking got louder.

"If Skipper is standing on the rocks,

44

that means the lighthouse is over there. So we need to go *this* way. Away from the rocks." He picked up the oars again and began to row.

"Keep barking, Skipper," Sky called. "You're helping us!"

Skipper was puzzled. He couldn't see his friend, and he could only just hear

her. But if he could hear a kitten, that meant she was really close to the rocks. He barked louder.

"Just keep barking," Sky mewed, as Joe steered the boat the other way.

Suddenly a bright light burst through the fog, sending a shining yellow beam into the sky.

"Look!" Sky mewed. "The lighthouse is working again!"

"Hurrah!" Skipper woofed. He was so excited, he almost fell off the rock he was standing on. "Well done, Mac!"

"Now I know we're definitely going in the right direction," said Joe, although he was frightened when he saw how close to the rocks they were. "Don't worry, Sky. We'll be home very soon."

He began to row as fast as he could.

Sky stood at the front of the boat and peered into the fog. She could just make out the harbour and the jetty ahead of them.

"Are you still there, Sky?" woofed Skipper from the rocks.

"We're nearly at the jetty," Sky mewed back. She could only just hear Skipper now because Joe had rowed past the lighthouse.

Skipper jumped down from the rocks, just as Mac came out of the lighthouse. "Skipper, where are you?" he called. "I've replaced the bulb."

"I've got to make sure Sky is OK!" Skipper barked. And he raced across the cliffs towards the harbour.

"Skipper, come back!" Mac called. "You might get lost in the fog."

But Skipper didn't stop. He had to go and find Sky!

Sky purred loudly as she saw the jetty loom out of the fog. "We're home, Joe," she miaowed in delight. As the boat moved closer to the jetty, Sky saw a small brown shape waiting for them. "It's Skipper!" she mewed.

Skipper ran anxiously up and down the jetty, watching the boat. Then he heard some people running behind him. He looked round. It was Mac, with Joe's dad.

"Joe!" Mr Kirby called. He looked rather cross. "Your mum and I were getting very worried about you. You

know you're not supposed to go out in the boat on your own!"

"Sorry, Dad," said Joe. "I just wanted to go fishing." He reached out and grabbed the side of the jetty to pull the boat nearer. Then he tied up the boat and lifted Sky on to the jetty.

She ran straight over to Skipper and rubbed her head against the puppy's warm, furry shoulder. "Oh, Skipper! I am so glad to see you!"

Skipper gave Sky a big lick on her pink nose.

Joe's dad saw the kitten, and looked very surprised. "What is Sky doing here?"

"She came fishing with me!" Joe said. "It was fun at first. But then we got lost in the fog."

"How did you find your way back?" asked Mr Kirby.

"Oh, that was easy," Sky purred. "It was all thanks to Skipper!"

"The lighthouse wasn't working," Joe said. "Luckily Skipper was out on the rocks. I could hear him barking, so I knew which way to go."

Mac smiled and patted Skipper's head. "Well done, Skipper," he said. "That's just what a lighthouse puppy should do!"

"You're a hero," mewed Sky.

The puppy looked very pleased. "Am I?" he woofed.

"Yes," purred Sky. "You're the best lighthouse puppy in the whole world!"

*

51

It was the following day. The fog had gone, and it was sunny and warm. Skipper and Sky sat by the harbour, watching the fishermen get ready to go out in the boats.

Skipper had something very important to show Sky. "Look at my medal," he woofed proudly. "Mac gave it to me this morning."

Sky admired the gold medal on Skipper's collar. "It's very shiny," she mewed.

"It says that I'm the Official Lighthouse Puppy," Skipper explained, wagging his tail.

"I'm glad you got a medal," Sky purred. "You helped me *twice* yesterday. First when I was stuck in the net, then when Joe and I got lost in the fog. You're my best friend, Skipper!"

"And you're *my* best friend," Skipper woofed.

The fishermen were ready to go now. Joe's dad jumped on board the *Jolly Jack* with a cheerful wave.

Skipper and Sky watched as the boats began to chug out of the harbour. "Don't you want to go to sea today?" Skipper asked.

Sky looked around the harbour. Joe was sitting on the wall, waving to his dad and eating a big yellow ice cream. The sun was hot on Sky's fur, and her tummy was full. She'd had fish for her breakfast, and there would be more fresh fish to eat when the boats came back.

"Why would I want to go to sea?" she
mewed at last. "I like dry land best!"

Look out for more brilliant

Best Friends

books

Amber and Alfie

Amber is a red squirrel who loves eating nuts – and anything else she can find! Her best friend, Alfie, is a little kitten who loves helping out at the railway station.

Amber will go anywhere to find some tasty food, so when Alfie spots her sneaking on to a train, he knows there will be trouble! And soon the two friends are on an exciting adventure that takes them far away from home . . .

Look out for more brilliant

books

Blossom and Beany

Blossom the piglet is feeling very sorry for herself. Just because she's small, her brothers and sisters won't play with her! Blossom has to play on her own, splashing around in puddles.

One day she finds a duck playing in her favourite puddle. Beany doesn't think Blossom is too small. In fact, she's the perfect size for a big farmyard adventure . . .

Look out for more brilliant

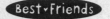

books

Carrot and Clover

Carrot is a little rabbit who lives in Becky's garden with his best friend Clover, a fluffy yellow chick. Every morning, Becky gives them their breakfast – then she goes out of the gate, and doesn't come back until teatime.

Carrot and Clover have never been outside the gate – let alone to school, where Becky spends the day! One day they decide to follow her – and find a whole new world waiting for them . . .